BUzzin'
with Kindness

SOPhia Z. DOmogala

Illustrations by Dwight Nacaytuna

To order additional copies of this book, contact:
Xlibris Corporation
1-888-795-4274
www.Xlibris.com
Orders@Xlibris.com

To my husband, Daniel, and my children, Michal, Krystyna, and Kathryn, and in memory of my parents, Anna and Walter, for their immeasurable inspiration.

Once upon a time, there were ten bees buzzing and flying in Mrs. Busy's classroom. The beautiful bees were colorful. The bees made lots of buzzing sounds. The bees were buzzing up in the air, upside down, sideways, and around. They were bumping into one another. The bees were all having lots of fun.

2

All of a sudden, the bees started to crash into one another. One of the bees said, "You crashed into me, and you hurt me."

Another bee said, "What do you say?"

A third bee said, "You hurt my wing."

"Well," said the first bee, "you hurt me too. When you hurt someone, what do you say?"

"I do not have to say anything."

"Say you are sorry. You hurt me."

"No," said the bee.

"Say you are sorry."

"OK, I am sorry for knocking you down and hurting your wing. It was an accident. I did not mean to kick you with my stinger and hurt your wing. I will fix your wing."

"No, wings cannot be fixed. My wing is broken."

The second bee said, "Sorry, sorry, sorry, oh, so sorry."

"That was kind of you to say that. You are being so kind when you say you are sorry for hurting my wing. Do not do it again."

"Oh! We are happy bees. We are buzzing around in Mrs. Busy's classroom."

"We are super bees."
One of the bees said, "In case we push, bump, or hurt one another again, will we say 'Move it, get out of my way, get away from me,' or do we use kind words to one another? What do you think?"
The third bee said, "We will use kind words to one another, such as 'Sorry' or 'Excuse me.'"

"Flying is fun," said the bees.
"Here we go again."
Suddenly, one of the bees accidentally bumped into a little girl. The little girl tried to hit the bee hard with her hand.
That bee said, "I am not a happy bee. The little girl tried to hit me."
The other bee said, "I will sting her."
"No," said the second bee.

All the bees are buzzing around in the classroom. The bees are flying in the air and making buzzing sounds, *buzzzzzzz*, as loud as they can. The noise keeps getting louder and louder and louder. *Buzzzzz*.

"What do we say when we are buzzing too loud or talking too loud in the classroom?"

One of the bees answered, "Please stop! And use your indoor voice. We must not buzz too loud. We are disturbing the teacher and the children. We must behave
and buzz softly."

"Here we are, just flying and buzzing in the air."
One bee said to the other, "I am not talking to you.
You took my space."
"Get out of my way," said the second bee.
The first bee said, "No. I hate you."

The second bee said, "That is not nice. You are not
being kind to me."
The first bee said, "I do not care."
The second bee said, "You should be kind and help
me find a space to fly around."

"No! No!" said the third bee. "Get away from me. I want to fly into the little boy's nose."

The first bee said, "You cannot fly into the little boy's nose. You will sting him."

"Oh! Yes, I can," said the third bee. "Watch me."

So the third bee flew into the little boy's noise. The little boy started to scream. The first bee said, "You must be a kind bee and not hurt the little boy. Tell the little boy you want to be his friend, and you will not sting him."

"OK," said the third bee. "I want you to be my friend, and I will not sting you."

"We are having fun up here, flying around."
"Oops, we knocked down some books on some of the children's feet."
"Oh my!" said one of the bees. "What do I say to the children?"
All the bees buzzed, "We are sorry, and we will help pick up the books."

16

One of the children kicked some books all over the classroom. Mrs. Busy was upset that the child kicked the books all around the floor.
She told the children to stop and not to kick the books. Mrs. Busy said, "What do you say when you do things that you are not supposed to do in the classroom?"

18

Mrs. Busy went next to the children. She said, "What do you say when you kick the books?"

The children said, "We hate books."

Mrs. Busy asked, "Are you using your kind words?"

Again Mrs. Busy said, "What do you say, boys and girls?"

The children said, "We will pick up the books and put them back on the bookshelf where they belong."

Mrs. Busy said, "You are using your kind words. That is wonderful."

When Mrs. Busy was not looking, the bees decided to fly around again. While the bees were flying, another child pushed two children into the closet. Mrs. Busy saw it and said to the children, "That is not a kind thing to do to one another. This is not kind at all. What do you say?"

Each of the children said, "We will help our friends get up and will not push them. We do not do this to our friends."

The children in Mrs. Busy's class started to say nasty things to one another. When Mrs. Busy heard the children, she immediately said, "We are not using our kind words to our friends. What do you think we should say to one another?"

The children said, "Let's have fun and play nice."
The children said, "We are all friends in school."
Mrs. Busy said, "Remember, try to use kind words, do not use bad words, we share, we help one another, we try hard to do our best, and we are good listeners. Now let's open the window to let the bees out."
The children all helped open the windows to let the bees out.
Mrs. Busy said, "Well done, boys and girls. Wow! Everyone did a great job! A super job!"
The bees went buzzin' away.

CPSIA information can be obtained at www.ICGtesting.com
Printed in the USA
BVIW12n1447040915
416195BV00004B/1